Witch's Cat

by RUTH CHEW

Illustrated by the author

Cover illustration by Rudy Nappi

D1125462

LITTLE APPLE
PAPERBACK

SCHOLASTIC INC.

New York   Toronto   London   Auckland   Sydney

ISBN 0-590-48341-2

12 11 10 9 8 7 6 5 4 3 2   4 5 6 7 8 9/9

Printed in the U.S.A.   40

First Scholastic printing, September 1994

For Shelly Robinson

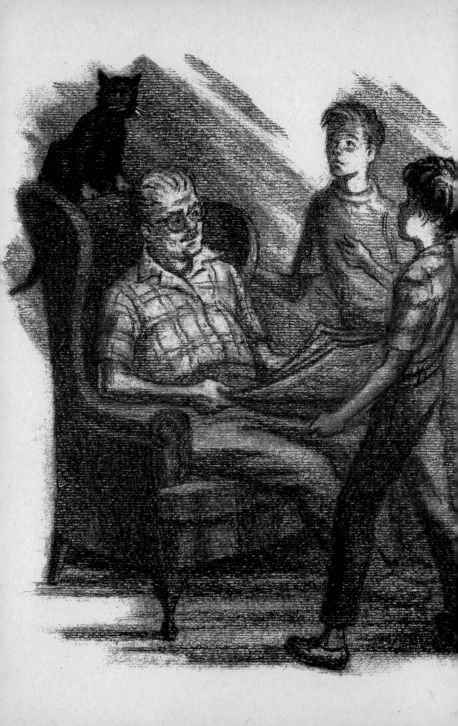

1

"Holly, look!" Matthew pointed to the shiny black cat perched on the high back of their grandfather's chair.

The cat stretched all over. Now they could see that his whiskers and all four of his paws were snowy white. Slowly he closed one of his bright green eyes. Holly thought he was winking at her.

Holly and Matthew had come to stay with their grandparents, the Dorritys, in Brooklyn. Their mother and father were away for a few days.

Mrs. Dorrity came down from upstairs.

"What's the cat's name, Granny?" Holly asked.

Mrs. Dorrity laughed. "Your grandfather calls him Albert."

"Why, Grandpa?" Matthew wanted to know.

"Because," Mr. Dorrity said, "he's the smartest cat I ever saw. I named him after Albert Einstein, the smartest scientist I ever heard of."

"I put your things in the back bedroom, Matthew," his grandmother told him. "Holly can have the middle room. You'd better go up and unpack. I'll get supper ready." She went to the kitchen.

Holly started upstairs. The black cat streaked past her and raced to the floor above. The children followed, but, by the time they reached the top of the stairs, the cat was out of sight.

They were in a narrow hall.

"Let's explore." Matthew started to walk toward the front of the old house.

"Matt," Holly reminded him, "didn't Granny tell us to unpack?"

The two of them went into a room halfway down the hall.

The suitcase with Holly's clothes was on the bed. Matthew was two years older than his sister. He helped her unpack. Then they both went to the back bedroom. The door was open. Holly peeked in. She grabbed her brother's arm and put her finger to her lips.

Matthew stared. There was a big bookcase in the room. Three books were open on the floor. The black cat was lying on his stomach. With one white paw he held the largest book in place. With another he was turning the pages.

2

Creak! Matthew stepped on a squeaky board in the old floor.

Albert jumped to his feet and began shoving the books around. The cat leaped into the air. Then he began to chase his tail as if he were a kitten.

Holly picked up the books and went to put them back into the bookcase.

Albert stopped chasing his tail and walked over to her. He began to purr. Suddenly he bumped his head against her leg.

Holly was so startled that she dropped the biggest book.

Matthew rushed to grab it, but he slipped on a little rug and slid across the bare floor. He held on to the end of the bed to keep from crashing into the radiator. Two wooden slats fell from the bed frame.

Moments later Mrs. Dorrity came into the room. "What are you children doing? I thought the kitchen ceiling was going to fall on my head!"

Now Mr. Dorrity, out of breath and holding on to the cat with both hands, came puffing in. "Guess who I caught sneaking down the hall?" He looked at the book on the floor. "Albert thinks books are something to play with. We'll have to put a hook on this door to keep him out." He took the cat downstairs.

Mrs. Dorrity went back to the kitchen.

Holly helped her brother unpack.

Matthew kept whistling under his breath.

When Mr. Dorrity came back with tools, Matthew stopped whistling and helped his grandfather put a hook and eye on each side of the door at the right height for Matthew and Holly to reach them.

Holly went to set the table. Supper was ready when her brother and her grandfather came downstairs.

Between bites of roast chicken, Holly asked, "How long have you had Albert, Grandpa?"

"Just since last Tuesday," Mr. Dorrity said. "We found him sleeping in your grandmother's herb garden."

"He's a nice cat, really," Mrs. Dorrity said.

"We just have to keep him out of our books," her husband reminded her.

"Maybe he wants to read them," Matthew said.

This was exactly what Holly had been thinking. But when her grandfather burst out laughing, she was glad she hadn't said it.

3

After supper they all went out into the little backyard. The cat came out after them.

A swing dangled from an enormous pear tree. The cat made a flying leap and landed on the swing seat. He sat there swaying gently back and forth.

Mr. Dorrity rubbed his chin. "Albert really ought to be in a circus."

"Maybe he ran away from one," Mrs. Dorrity said.

The pear tree shaded most of the garden. Holly saw a lot of plants like the ones in her backyard at home. "I thought this was an herb garden, Granny."

"Herbs need sun." Mrs. Dorrity pointed to the corner of the garden farthest from the pear tree. "My herb garden is over there."

Holly and Matthew followed their grandmother over to the patch of sunny ground. It was crowded with all sorts of plants. Some of them had feathery leaves, and others had shiny ones. One even had curly purple leaves.

Mrs. Dorrity showed the children some spiky blue flowers. "I make one kind of tea from the leaves of these and a different tea from the little white daisies over there."

Matthew bent over a plant with bright blue flowers and hairy leaves. "What do you use these flowers for, Gran?"

"I make them into candy," Mrs. Dorrity told him. "And the leaves are good for lemonade!"

Mr. Dorrity joined them. "I always thought herbs were just those dried things in little jars." He held a green leaf under Holly's nose. "Smells like chewing gum, doesn't it?" He picked another leaf. "And this is probably what brought Albert to the garden."

"Catnip?" Matthew asked.

"You guessed it," his grandfather said. "He was fast asleep when I first saw him. He must have been drunk on catnip."

Holly turned to look at Albert, who had stopped swinging but was still sitting on the swing. She could see that the cat's ears were flat against his head. He seemed to know that Mr. Dorrity was talking about him.

Silently the cat jumped down from the swing and trotted to the kitchen door. It was closed but not clicked shut. With one white paw Albert pulled the door open and slipped into the house.

4

The swing jiggled for a little while after the cat jumped off. Matthew walked over to it. "Where's Albert?"

"He went into the house," Holly said. "He didn't like Grandpa saying he got drunk on catnip."

Mr. Dorrity laughed. "You mean I hurt his feelings? I'll have to be more careful after this."

Mrs. Dorrity opened the back door. "Come indoors, children. It's getting late."

She held the door open until everyone was inside.

Mr. Dorrity looked around the kitchen. "I wonder where that cat is. At least we know he's not playing with the books in the back bedroom." He yawned. "Well, I'm off to bed. Anybody have a hug for me?"

Holly and Matthew both went to hug their grandfather.

Mrs. Dorrity kissed them goodnight. "Sleep well," she said.

The children went upstairs. They kept looking for the cat, but they didn't see him anywhere. The old house was spooky at night. A little light came from a night-light in the bathroom.

Matthew snapped on the light in Holly's room halfway down the hall. He walked into the room and looked around. "No cat here."

"There are no books in here either," Holly said. "Maybe I can find something to read in your room."

They went around the bend in the hall to Matthew's room.

The door was closed, but there was a dim light showing under it.

For a moment the two children stood quite still. Then Holly took a deep breath and pushed the door open.

Albert was lying on the floor with a book open in front of him. A little square flashlight was set on its side to shine on the page of the book as the cat turned the pages.

5

"That's my flashlight! He's wearing out the battery." Matthew switched it off and put it into his pocket.

Holly turned on the ceiling light and bent down to pick up the heavy book.

The cat put both front paws on the open pages. "Don't lose my place."

Holly and Matthew stared at the cat. Then Matthew picked up an envelope from the desk. "Will this do for a book-mark?"

Holly put the envelope in the book to mark the cat's place. She put the book on the bottom shelf of the big bookcase. "Just be careful with the books, Albert. Grandpa thinks you're playing with them."

"It's not easy for me to take them out and put them back," the cat said. "Maybe you two could help me."

"Must you read the books?" Matthew asked. "Grandpa and I went to a lot of trouble to keep you from getting into them. How did you get in here, anyway?"

Albert stood up and stretched. "If you hook the door, I'll show you."

Matthew shut the door and hooked it on the inside.

"Out of my way!" the cat ordered.

Both children moved away from the door.

Albert measured the distance with his eyes. Then he jumped up and knocked the hook out of the eye. He landed on the floor with a thump.

In almost no time Mrs. Dorrity came pattering down the hall and tapped on the door. "What's going on in there? I heard a bang. I thought you children were going to bed. Does your mother let you stay up so late?"

The cat ran under the bed.

Holly opened the door. "It's my fault, Granny. I wanted a book to read."

Mrs. Dorrity went to the bookcase. "Here's one I always loved." She pulled out a battered book with a red cloth binding, and handed it to Holly. "Don't stay up too late with it. By the way, has either of you seen that cat? I want to give him his supper."

Before either of the children could answer, Albert tiptoed out from his hiding place and went to rub against Mrs. Dorrity's leg. She picked him up and held him against her cheek. "Silly cat," she said. "We all know you weren't drunk on catnip. You're much too smart for that." She took him downstairs to the kitchen with her.

Matthew took out his flashlight and got down on his hands and knees in front of the bookcase to look at the title of the big book Albert had been reading. "Holly," he whispered, "take a look at this!"

Holly had already started the book her grandmother had given her. Now she lay on her stomach to look at the name of the book the cat found so interesting. "*Magic from the Common Garden Herb*," she read.

"We'd better watch that cat," Matthew said.

6

Holly went to her own room to read before taking her shower. She sat on her bed, but before she could open the book, her brother came into the room. "What's the matter, Matt?"

"Holly, was that cat really talking? Or am I nuts?" Matthew asked.

"He was talking," Holly said. "You know Grandpa said he was the smartest cat he ever saw."

"Grandpa laughed when I said Albert wanted to read," Matthew reminded her.

"Maybe Albert doesn't just want to," Holly said. "I think he does read."

"Then why doesn't he tell Gramps he won't hurt the books?" Matthew asked.

Holly thought about this. "Grandpa doesn't believe in magic. He might have a heart attack if Albert spoke to him. Even you thought you were crazy. Albert is a nice cat. He likes Grandpa and doesn't want to hurt him."

"I hope you're right," Matthew said.

At this moment Mrs. Dorrity walked in and saw that Holly was holding the book. "I shouldn't have given that to you tonight, dear," she said. "You'll never get to bed. I'll keep it for you till tomorrow." She took the book. "You don't have time to take a bath. Maybe you two should take showers instead." She left the room.

Matthew went to his room to get undressed. He rushed to the bathroom before Holly could get there first.

When at last Holly was in bed, she had a hard time getting to sleep. Finally she got up and tiptoed over to the tall bay windows at one end of the room.

The center window was open. Holly peeked through the venetian blind and looked down into the backyard. A yellow moon was rising over the big pear tree.

Holly saw something moving around in the corner of the garden where her grandmother grew her herbs. It seemed to be an animal. Maybe it was a rat!

When her eyes became used to the moonlight, she saw that it was a black cat with white paws. He was nibbling at the plants.

Grandpa was right after all! Holly said to herself. Albert was crazy about catnip.

The cat backed out of the patch of plants and trotted to the kitchen door.

Holly went back to bed. In a few minutes she was fast asleep.

7

The early morning sunlight streaming through the cracks in the venetian blind woke Holly. She jumped out of bed and pulled the blind all the way up. Now a gentle breeze came in her open window. Holly went to the bathroom to wash her face and brush her teeth.

She came back to get dressed. As she leaned over to roll up the legs of her jeans and tie her shoelaces, a furry head bumped against her leg.

"Good morning, Albert," Holly said.

The cat purred. Holly scooped him up and held him against her cheek. She

waited for him to say something, but Albert just went on purring.

Holly wondered if she had dreamed
that the cat was talking last night.

Then she heard a purry whisper.
"Wake your brother! He has his door
hooked. I want to get in there."

Holly remembered that Matthew was
worried about what the cat was up to.
She held on to Albert and took him down
the hall toward her brother's room.

Before she reached the door, Matthew
opened it. He was wearing a bathrobe
and slippers. When he stepped into the
hall, he skidded on something and almost fell.

"For goodness' sake, be careful!" the cat said. "Look what you've done to my samples!"

Albert wriggled out of Holly's grasp and landed softly on all four of his white paws. With his mouth, the cat began to pick up tiny sprigs of herbs that were laid in neat piles on the shiny wood floor.

Albert carried one of the piles into Matthew's room. He put it near a wall. Then he went to get another pile. "Do you think you two could pick up these things without bruising them?" he asked.

"Of course." Matthew took four sheets of notepaper from the desk and gave two to Holly. They each used one sheet of paper to push a pile of leaves onto another sheet. Soon all the piles were lined up along a wall in Matthew's bedroom. He went to the bathroom to brush his teeth.

Albert trotted over to the bookcase. He put his paw on the book he was looking at the night before. "How about getting this out for me, Holly?"

Holly pulled the book out of the bookcase and put it open on the floor near the piles of leaves.

The cat turned the pages of the book until he came to one with pictures of plants. He began to compare his herbs with the pictures in the book.

8

"Holly, come here!" Matthew stood barefoot in the doorway of his room. The cat was busy trying to match his herb samples with the pictures in the book.

Holly walked over to her brother. He handed her one of his red corduroy slippers. "Take a look at the bottom of this."

Holly saw that the sole of the slipper was smeared with some sort of green slime.

"I can't get this gunk off," Matthew said. "I have to get dressed now."

"Give me the slippers. I'll see what I can do." Holly took the slippers to her room.

She heard her grandfather calling, "Matthew! Holly! Breakfast time!"

Holly pulled open the top drawer of the dresser, stuffed the red slippers into it, and closed the drawer tight.

Something smelled delicious. Holly went downstairs to the kitchen.

"Where's Matthew?" Mrs. Dorrity asked. "Your grandfather is making waffles."

"Matt isn't dressed yet," Holly said.

Mr. Dorrity put a waffle on her plate and poured batter into the waffle iron. "Don't let this burn," he said to his wife. "I'm going to get that boy. You have to eat waffles when they're hot." He rushed out of the room.

Mrs. Dorrity smiled. "Your grandfather gets very excited when he cooks anything."

As soon as the waffle was ready, Mrs. Dorrity took it out of the waffle iron and put it into the oven.

Mr. Dorrity came downstairs with the cat under one arm and the book under the other. Matthew followed him into

the kitchen. His grandmother gave him
the waffle she was keeping warm.

"Good thing I went upstairs," Mr.
Dorrity said. "Albert was into the books
again. This is a very interesting old cookbook. I bought it at a garage sale. I'm
sure I'll never find another copy. I'll just
have to lock it up. Albert must be after
a recipe for catnip tea."

Mr. Dorrity laughed and put the cat on the floor. He took the book into the dining room and locked it in a cabinet. Then he came back into the kitchen. "Anybody ready for another waffle?"

Both Matthew and Holly were hungry for more. Their grandfather poured batter into the waffle iron.

Holly felt sorry for Albert. He was sitting quite still, and his white whiskers drooped.

Mrs. Dorrity leaned over to scratch the cat behind the ears. Then she filled his bowl with leftover roast chicken and put it down beside him.

9

After he finished his breakfast Albert
went upstairs. Holly and Matthew followed him. The black cat went all the
way down the hall to Matthew's room.

Mr. Dorrity had hooked the door.

Albert leaped up and knocked the
hook out of the eye with one forepaw.
At the same time he used both hind legs
to kick the door open. The cat sailed into
the room and landed in front of the little
piles of herbs.

"Grandpa's right," Holly said. "You really do belong in the circus."

"You're terrific, Albert!" Matthew told him.

Albert's whiskers perked up. "I've had practice." He checked all the little piles. "I ought to keep them separate. I still don't know if I have the herbs I need."

Matthew shut the door. He took some envelopes off the desk. "You could put a different herb in each envelope and write the names on them."

"I've learned to read," the cat said, "but I haven't figured out how to write yet."

"You can tell us what to write and we'll do it for you," Holly told him.

Matthew and Holly set to work and wrote names like Chervil and Tansy on the envelopes. Albert inspected each pile of leaves, looking carefully and sniffing even more carefully. Then he showed them which herb to put into each envelope.

"Don't let them get mixed with each other," the cat warned them.

"What are you going to do with the herbs?" Holly asked.

The tip of Albert's tail twitched. "I've seen herbs boiled and burned and scattered to make different kinds of magic. It's what herbs you use together and how you blend them and the words you speak that make the difference. But I never learned the secret. I was going to find out from your grandfather's book."

"Grandpa said it was a cookbook." Matthew picked up the envelopes and put them on the desk. "They're here whenever you want them, Albert."

The cat's whiskers drooped. "Maybe that's why the book said 'Use to flavor soups and fish.' Why would anybody want to flavor fish?"

Holly opened the door and stepped into the hall. "I'm going to ask Granny for her book." She looked at the cat. "Albert, what's the matter with you?"

The cat's green eyes gleamed and his white whiskers bristled. All his shiny black fur was standing on end. He sniffed the air. "I thought I smelled something I never smelled in this house before, but it was very faint, and I couldn't be sure. It's getting stronger and stronger."

The cat sniffed the floor. Still sniffing, he crept silently out the door and down the hall.

Holly and Matthew tiptoed after him.

10

Albert went into Holly's room and started sniffing everywhere.

Matthew and Holly watched him from the doorway. The cat stopped in front of the dresser and stood on his hind legs to sniff each drawer. He jumped onto the dresser and leaned over to sniff at the one on the top.

Albert turned to look at the children. His green eyes seemed enormous. "Magic!" he said softly. "Powerful magic! What is in there?"

"Matt's bedroom slippers." Holly went over to the drawer and pulled out the two red corduroy slippers.

At once one slipper began to get bigger. Holly dropped the other one so she could hold on to the growing one with both hands. It kept getting bigger. She put the slipper on her foot over her shoe, and stood on it to keep it down. But the slipper went on growing.

Soon it was big enough for Holly to

put her other foot in the slipper too. Then it was big enough to sit down in.

"Move over, Holly. After all, it's my slipper." Matthew stepped in and sat down beside his sister.

The cat had been watching from the top of the dresser. Now he jumped down and landed in Holly's lap. "Stop growing, Slipper!" he commanded. "You're quite big enough now."

The slipper stopped growing.

"When you're dealing with magic," Albert explained, "it's important to make sure the enchanted object knows who is Master of the Magic."

"What makes you Master of the Magic?" Holly wanted to know.

"I gathered the herbs that are smeared together on the bottom of this slipper," Albert explained. "They produced a certain mixture Nell Fisher always found very handy."

"Who is Nell Fisher?" Holly asked.

"A good friend of mine," the cat said. "She never would tell me the secret of her magic, but by accident your brother stumbled onto it."

"Then why isn't Matt the Master of the Magic?" Holly asked.

"He didn't gather the herbs," Albert said. "If I knew which herbs are crushed together, maybe I could make more of the mixture, but I'd have to know just what time of day it was, the phase of the moon, how much of each herb was used, how much pressure was applied, and what the magic words were."

The cat thought for a moment. "We'll have to make do with the mixture we have here," he told the children. "There's no time to lose! Nell Fisher is in trouble, and we have to help her."

11

"What are we waiting for?" Matthew said. "Let's go, Albert!"

The cat sat up straight in Holly's lap. "Slipper," he said, "we have to travel back in time to find Nell Fisher. Can you do this?"

For almost a full minute the slipper did not move.

"What's the matter?" Holly asked.

"Time travel is a special skill," Albert told her, "and the slipper is new to magic."

The slipper gave a little jiggle.

Holly stroked the soft red corduroy. "You're so bright," she whispered. "I'm sure you can learn."

Very slowly the slipper floated up into the air and headed for the open window. Holly was sure the window was too small for them to go through, but it became bigger and bigger. The windowsill was as wide as a highway by the time they sailed over it into the open air.

Everything outdoors was enormous too.

"Matt," Holly said. "How did everything become so big so fast?"

"I think we became small," her brother told her.

"That's clever of the slipper," the cat said. "We're so small nobody notices us."

The slipper was rising straight up now. It travelled so fast that, before they knew it, they could hardly see the streets and houses down below.

Very soon the daylight turned to darkest night. The Earth they had left became smaller and smaller until it was just a blue ball whirling through space. Then it was so small that it looked like a star. The two children lost sight of it among the many bigger stars that they rushed past.

For a while they seemed to be lost in a crowd of stars, all different sizes and colors, and all going different ways.

Then, far, far off, a small blue star came in sight. Matthew grabbed his sister's arm. "Holly! We must have gone in a circle. That looks like our Earth!"

The sky was getting lighter. It seemed to be very early in the morning. They sank down and down. At last the slipper

landed gently on the water of a narrow winding river.

Holly patted the side of the slipper. She was surprised that it felt hard, not like corduroy at all!

The two children and the cat looked around. They were sitting on the seat of a strange wooden boat with both ends curving up into high points. Around them dragonflies darted over the water.

There was a hole in each side of the boat with an oar poking through it. Matthew grabbed one oar, and Holly took hold of the other.

"Watch how you handle those!" Albert jumped to the front of the boat. "I don't want to be splashed."

12

Boats are always rowed backward. Matthew and Holly had to keep turning their heads to see where they were going. Albert sat in the front of the boat and told them what was up ahead.

"Watch out!" the cat said. "We're coming to a big rock in the water."

They steered around the rock and rowed between tall green reeds.

A cool breeze blew around them. A bird chirped. The sun came up from behind a long row of rocky hills.

"Look, Matt!" Holly pointed to a mother sheep with a little lamb. They were nibbling wild grass in a field on one side of the river.

On the other side was a deep wood.

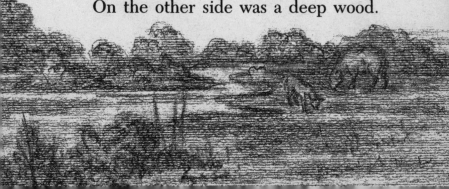

"That looks like a good place to camp," Matthew said.

They rowed around a bend in the river. A grove of willows grew at the edge of the water. Before they reached the trees, a harsh voice said, "Drat! You've scared the fish!"

Matthew and Holly stopped rowing, but the boat drifted closer to the trees.

Someone was sitting on a branch that hung over the water, fishing with a long pole. At first the children couldn't tell if it was a man or a woman.

Albert became very excited. "Nell Fisher! What are you doing here?"

"Fishing. What else would I be doing?"

Now Holly and Matthew saw that it was a tall bony woman with big hands and feet. She had scraggly gray hair, dark piercing eyes, a long pointed nose, a sharp chin, and a thin crooked mouth.

The woman edged her way along the branch until she could slide off onto the ground. She stood up. Her clothes were torn and dirty. She waded into the water, lifted the cat out of the boat, and held him against her bony neck. "I never thought I'd see you again, Cat. Those clods told me they were going to drown you. They tried to drown me too, but I found an underwater tunnel and escaped." She stroked Albert. "You seem unharmed. Maybe that brew I rubbed on your nose helped."

"It smelled terrible," Albert told her. "I could hardly breathe. And when those people held me under the water, I sank. I woke up later in a bed of herbs. I want you to meet Holly and Matthew. It was their grandmother who grew the herbs. They travelled with me from a place unknown to people here."

Still holding the cat, Nell Fisher curtsied to Holly and Matthew. They took off their shoes, rolled up the legs of their jeans, and climbed out of the boat. Then they dragged it ashore.

"Albert told us you're in trouble," Holly said. "We want to help you."

"Who's Albert?" Nell Fisher asked. "Oh, you mean Cat?"

"Our grandpa says he's the cleverest cat he ever saw, so he named him after a clever man," Matthew told her.

Nell Fisher's crooked mouth cracked into a grin. "He's a nice cat," she said. "But I always thought he was stupid."

Albert bumped his furry head against her bony shoulder and purred.

13

Nell Fisher pulled a string of small fish out of the river. "It's lucky I caught these before you folk came splashing along. Who's ready for breakfast?"

The waffles seemed to have been eaten long ago. Everybody was hungry.

Nell Fisher took Matthew, Holly, and Albert into the woods and showed them her campground. There was a small fire burning in a hollow in the ground.

Nell cooked the fish whole by pushing sticks through them and laying them across the hollow where the fire burned. She kept turning the sticks as the fish cooked.

"What happened to your pots and pans, Nell?" the cat asked.

"I don't know," Nell Fisher told him.
"After my neighbors took you away, they
set fire to my cottage and destroyed
everything in my herb garden. They
roped bags of stones around my waist
and tied my hands and feet. Then they
threw me into the river."

"Why did they do that?" Matthew
asked.

"It was really all my fault," Albert told
him. "Nell let me live with her and even
talked to me. Around here people who
keep cats are thought to be witches.
After a while, whenever anybody fell
into a ditch and hurt his leg or if a cow

stopped giving milk, people thought Nell had worked an evil spell."

"Isn't there a law here against killing someone just because you think she's a witch?" Matthew asked.

"Of course," Albert said. "This was a trial to see if Nell really was a witch. It's called Trial by Water. They tie up the suspect and throw her into deep water. If she sinks, she's innocent, because a witch would have magic to save herself from the water. If she doesn't sink, she's guilty. As punishment she is either hanged or burned."

"As long as none of these people see me," Nell Fisher said, "they believe I'm innocent, but if they see me alive and well, I'm in trouble."

The fish were brown and crisp now. Holly picked some big green leaves to use as plates.

"Why does everything taste so good

when you eat it with your fingers?" Matthew said.

"Maybe because there are no dishes to wash afterward," Holly told him.

After breakfast Nell Fisher led the children to a blackberry patch growing in a sunny little glade. "Watch out for the thorns," she warned them. "I don't have any herbs to put on scratches. And eat what you pick. They taste best right off the bush."

"That's what I try to tell Mom," Matthew said. "Blackberries get squishy when you try to keep them."

"I want to talk to Cat. Come back to the campground when you've had enough berries." Nell Fisher left the glade.

14

After they'd eaten their fill of blackberries, Holly and Matthew started to
follow a little path back to Nell Fisher's
campground. They came to a place
where the path became two paths.

"Too bad we didn't notice this on the
way here," Matthew said. "The paths
look so much alike that I don't know
which one we should take."

"We can take either," Holly told him.
"If we find it's the wrong one, we'll come
back and take the other."

They started along the path to the

right. When they had been walking for some time and had not come to Nell Fisher's campground, Matthew said, "We'd better go back and take the other path."

Holly put her finger to her lips. "Listen!"

They heard a crashing sound coming toward them. Matthew pulled his sister off the path and into the underbrush. They lay on their stomachs and peeked through the tangled leaves.

A reddish-brown deer with spreading antlers came bounding along the path. He was followed by a pack of hounds barking in deep, long tones.

Close behind the hounds galloped a group of horseback riders.

Suddenly the deer left the path and leaped away in a circle, going through the woods in the opposite direction from the dogs and the people. In their hurry to turn, the dogs and the horses banged into each other. One rider fell off.

He wore plain brown clothes and seemed to be a servant. He jumped to his feet and grabbed his horse's reins. "If you ask me, Nell Fisher is up to her tricks again."

A tall man in a beautiful red and gold jacket said, "How is that, Tom? I thought they found she wasn't a witch, so she's not to blame for all our troubles."

Tom pulled a lock of his hair. This made his head duck. "Beg pardon, my lord, but Nell's body was not found. She could be anywhere around here."

"If she is," the lord said, "we'll find her and take the proper steps. The hounds are baying again. Maybe they've picked up the scent." He galloped after the dogs. The rest of the hunting party followed him.

Holly and Matthew crawled out from under the bushes and raced back to the fork in the path. They took the path that led to Nell Fisher's campground.

Nell was waiting for them. "Hurry up! Cat has promised to take me for a boat ride."

15

The boat was right where they had left it on the bank near the willow trees. Nell Fisher helped Matthew and Holly push it into the water.

The cat jumped into the front of the boat. Nell Fisher took her place on the seat. Matthew and Holly sat one on each side of her and picked up the oars.

"Nell," Matthew said. "You'd better get down low in the boat, so no one can see you."

"I've a better idea," Albert said. "Nell could change herself into a frog."

"You forget I don't have any of my magic mixtures," Nell Fisher reminded him.

Holly patted the side of the boat. "Maybe Slipper can help."

The boat quivered as if a little breeze

had come up. A sweet voice said, "What's the matter with my hands?" Matt and Holly looked to see who had spoken.

A beautiful young woman was seated between the children. She had light brown hair that shone like gold in the sunlight and dark blue eyes with long lashes. Her hair was in two thick braids that reached to her waist, and her long blue gown was embroidered with daisies.

The woman was looking at her small white hands. "Very pretty," she said. "I hope they're as strong as usual."

"I don't think anyone will know you now, Nell," the cat said.

Nell Fisher raised one foot in the air. She looked at the soft pointed shoe that was tied to her foot with leather thongs. "I'm not used to these things."

A branch of a willow tree hung over

the boat. Nell Fisher stood up, grabbed hold of the branch, and swung herself up to sit on it. She stood up and held on to the branch above. "This gown is a nuisance." She tucked the hem of it into her belt. Now her dress was not so long and she could walk along the branch without holding on.

Holly was afraid she'd fall into the water, but Nell turned and came back. She slipped down to the lower branch, and from there dropped into her place between Matthew and Holly in the boat.

"I never knew you to be such a show-off, Nell," Albert said.

"I was just testing to see how I could move in these fancy clothes," she told him.

Holly looked down into the water beside the boat. She could see the leaves overhead and the blue sky and even her own face in the still water under the willow tree. "Trade places with me, Nell," she said. "And take a look at what's in the water here."

16

Holly moved to the middle of the boat.

Nell Fisher looked down into the still water at the side. For a minute she didn't say anything. Then she whispered, "Who's that?"

"That's you, Nell," the cat told her. "Who did you think it was?"

Holly and Matthew were both astonished to see Nell Fisher blinking tears from her eyes. "What's the matter?" Matthew asked.

"It's just," she said, "that I always wanted to look exactly like that."

Before any of them knew what was happening, a pack of dogs burst out of the forest, followed by a group of riders on horseback. Albert slid down into the boat and hid under the skirt of Nell Fisher's gown.

"Row, Holly!" Matthew whispered.

The two children started to row out into the middle of the river.

"Stop!" a voice commanded. "In the name of the lord of these lands." It was the voice of the groom who had fallen off his horse in the woods.

"Do as he says," Nell Fisher advised. "There are men with longbows ready to shoot their arrows at us."

The children stopped rowing.

The tall man in the red and gold jacket rode his horse into the water. When the man saw Nell Fisher, he took off his red velvet cap and bowed low over his horse's neck. "I am Robert, Earl of Garrick," he said. "Who are you, fair lady, and how do you come here?"

"My name is Eleanor of Fiswell," Nell told him. "My friends and I have travelled far and heard of your noble deeds. I pray you to allow us to continue our journey."

The earl stared at Nell Fisher. "I cannot permit you to continue alone and defenseless," the earl said. "You must

come to my castle where you will be safe."

"My lord," Nell Fisher said. "These children are in my care. I must not leave them."

"If there were room for them on my horse, I'd take them with me." The earl leaned over and pulled Nell out of the boat. He placed her in front of him on the big horse. "As you see, there's only just enough room for you here." He smiled. "But your friends will be most welcome at Castle Garrick. It's five miles down the river." He pointed in the direction from which they had rowed earlier in the day. Then he put spurs to his horse and rode back to the riverbank.

17

When the earl was back on shore
again, he took a little curved hunting
horn from his belt and blew two sharp
blasts. Nell Fisher sat on his horse in
front of him. She held her head high and
seemed to be enjoying herself.

At the sound of the horn, the people
on horseback lined up behind the earl.
The dogs followed.

Holly and Matthew sat in the boat and
watched until the company of horsemen

and the dogs went back into the forest, taking Nell Fisher with them.

"I suppose now we can go home," Matthew said. "Nell Fisher seems to have found her Prince Charming. Only somehow I don't like the guy."

"He's awful," Holly agreed. "What do we do now, Albert?"

The cat was still on the bottom of the boat. "Lucky the earl didn't notice me. Everybody around here knows I'm Nell's cat."

"Maybe the slipper could turn you into something else," Matthew suggested. "Wouldn't it be fun to be a bird for a change?"

"What makes you think it's fun to be a bird?" Albert said. "Watch one sometime. They're always on the lookout for danger."

Matthew laughed. "Slipper might turn you into a boy."

"Or a girl," Holly told the cat. "We have fun."

The cat shudderd. "I'd have to wear clothes, and eat with a fork."

Holly bent down to pet the cat. "It would only be for a little while, Silly!"

"Don't be too sure," Albert said. "Magic is dangerous. I might get stuck the way Nell is."

Holly stopped petting him. "What do you mean, Albert?"

"How is Nell Fisher stuck?" Matthew asked the cat.

Albert jumped onto the seat. "A witch cannot weep," he told the children. "They can pretend to cry, but they cannot really shed tears. When Nell looked at herself in the water, tears came into her eyes. Because of that she is no longer a witch and cannot go back to being one."

"But I thought she was tried as a

73

witch, and found innocent," Holly said.

"She didn't drown," Matthew reminded his sister.

"You tricked us, Albert," Holly said. "You never told us she was a witch!"

Albert stood up and stretched. "I never said she wasn't. But, witch or not, she's still my friend, and something tells me she still needs help."

Holly stroked the cat's back. She picked up an oar. "On to the castle, Matt!"

18

The boat followed the current going downstream. Matthew and Holly didn't have to row much. Most of the time they just steered.

The sun was high in the sky now. Albert stayed in the bottom of the boat. Now and then he peeked over the side.

They passed a number of sheep in the fields on one side of the river. A man holding a long stick with a curved end was watching over them.

When the boat came to a burned patch of ground, the cat said, "That's where Nell Fisher's cottage used to be."

"She told us it was her neighbors who burned it," Matthew said. "I don't see any neighbors."

Albert hid under the seat of the boat. "She meant the people in the town we're coming to."

Matthew and Holly rowed the boat around a bend of the river. Ahead of them they saw a number of houses with roofs of woven straw or slabs of slate.

Beyond the town a huge rock rose high out of the river. A gray stone castle with round towers and notched battlements was built on top of the rock.

"If nobody has knocked them down in

my absence," the cat said from under the seat, "you should be looking at Garrick Town and Castle Garrick."

"You're in danger here, Albert," Matthew said.

"If you wrap me in your shirt and let Holly carry me, people might not know I was a cat." Albert gave a cry that sounded like a baby's wail. "If anybody wants to know why you're without a shirt, tell them you're using it to keep me warm."

Holly and Matthew rowed the boat to the shore. They took off their shoes, tied the laces together, and hung them around their necks. Then they rolled up the legs of their jeans and stepped into the shallow water.

Matthew took off his T-shirt. Holly pulled the cat out from under the seat of the boat, rolled him in the baggy shirt, and carried him ashore.

Matthew put both hands on the boat. "Slipper," he whispered, "I know Albert claims to be Master of the Magic, but after all, you are my slipper, so would you please return to your old size, so I can put you into my pocket."

For a few seconds, nothing happened. Then Matthew found that he was holding the red corduroy slipper in his hands. He stuffed it into the side pocket of his jeans.

Holly was busy making sure that Albert could breathe under the shirt.

"I can't see," the cat said, "but it doesn't matter. My nose tells me where we are. There's a path above the riverbank that leads to the town."

19

Matthew and Holly took turns holding the cat while they put on their shoes.

Holly looked around. "Matt!" she whispered. "I can't see the boat anywhere! It must have drifted away and sunk."

"The boat's safe, Holly," Matthew said, "It's here in my pocket."

Holly poked a finger into his pocket and stroked the soft corduroy. Then she took the cat and climbed after her brother to the top of the bank.

They followed the path leading to the town. As they walked, the houses became closer together. From the path the children could look down and see docks along the waterfront with boats next to them. Beyond the docks the river curved around the castle rock.

On the other side of the river was the forest. Matthew pointed to where a horseman was galloping his horse across the river to a ramp near the docks. "It must be shallow there."

As Holly and Matthew watched, a pack of hounds came out of the forest and waited on the shore until another rider followed and ordered them into the water. Then the dogs swam across.

A gray-haired woman walking along the path stopped to watch. "You're strangers," she said. "That's the hunting party from the castle. And there's Earl Robert." She stared at the sight of Nell Fisher riding proudly in front of the earl. "He seems to have caught something other than a deer. Well, it's none of my business."

The rest of the hunting party came out

of the forest and splashed across the
river. The sun began to go down behind
the trees of the forest. The sky turned
pink and then gray. A cold wind began
to blow.

The woman looked at Matthew. "Who
are you, and what are you doing without
a shirt?"

Holly answered for him. "His name is
Matthew. I am his sister Holly. Matthew
lent his shirt to Albert here, who has no
clothes at all."

The cat let out a little cry.

Holly patted the shirt. "Sh-h-h!"

"Where are your parents?" the woman demanded.

"We don't know where our parents are," Matthew told her. "We're on our way to the castle. We're friends of the lady the earl has on his horse. We don't know the earl, but he has taken away our friend."

"As I said before, it isn't my business," the woman said, "but I do know the earl, and I don't like him. My name is Meg Turner, and I want to help you. You'll have a better chance of getting into the castle if you have a shirt. My cottage is down the road a bit. I think I have something you can wear. Come along."

20

Holly and Matthew followed Meg Turner to a small cottage. It was built of layers of mud and woven reeds and coated with white plaster. The roof was a thick thatch of mud covered with dry grass and leaves. The land around the cottage was separated from the neighbors' fields by ridges of earth.

It was twilight now and getting darker every minute. Meg Turner opened her door. "Come in, children," she said.

Matthew and Holly stepped into the house. It was just one room.

There was a small window in each

wall. The windows were criss-crossed with strips of wood, but there was no glass in them. It was dark outside now. The only light in the room came from a small fire glowing on a stone slab in the middle of the floor. The smoke escaped through a hole in the roof.

Meg Turner took a two-foot-long reed that had been dipped in fat and lit it from the fire. It burned like a candle.

She walked over to a large wicker trunk against one wall. "Come here, Matthew." She handed him the candle, opened the trunk, and took out a tunic. It was woven of unbleached black and white wool that looked speckly gray.

"This belonged to my son." Meg Turner took the candle. "He was no taller than you. Put it on."

Matthew slipped the tunic on over his head. It reached halfway between his waist and his knees.

"You'll need a sash." Meg Turner gave him one. Matthew knotted it around his waist. "Thank you, Mrs. Turner."

"No fancy Mistress Turner. Everyone calls me Meg," she said.

"Well, then, thank you, Meg. Now we'd better go to the castle." Matthew walked to the door and opened it. Holly followed him, holding the cat, who was still wrapped in Matthew's shirt.

They looked out at the blackest night they had ever seen. There were no lights in the houses and no street lamps. There was not even a moon.

Meg Turner closed the door. "It's too late. You can go to the castle in the morning. You must be hungry. What have you had to eat today?"

Holly thought for a moment. "Waffles, fish, and blackberries," she said.

Meg Turner put the candle in a holder on the table. She went to a cupboard on

the wall and took out a loaf of bread,
three rosy apples, a wedge of cheese,
and a jug of cider and put them on the
table.

Next she set out three pottery bowls
and filled them with soup from a large
pot steaming on the hearthstone.
"Would the baby like a bowl of porridge?" she asked.

"I think he'd do better with a cup of
milk," Matthew told her.

21

"Is there something the matter with the baby?" Meg Turner asked. "Holly seems to be hiding him."

"He's afraid to have people see him," Matthew said.

"Poor child." Meg Turner poured milk into a pottery mug and handed it to Holly. "What happened to his mother?"

"We don't know." Holly held the mug under the shirt the cat was wrapped in. She felt Albert's whiskers brush her hand as he lapped the milk. She had to keep tipping the mug as the cat drank.

"Put the baby to sleep on the bed over there." Meg Turner pointed to a pile of straw in one corner of the room. "Then you çan eat your supper in peace."

After Albert had finished his milk, Holly laid him down and came back to the table. Meg Turner cut thick slices of crusty bread to eat with the soup.

"Where is your son, whose shirt I'm wearing, Meg?" Matthew asked.

"Earl Robert dragged him off to war, along with my husband," Meg Turner said. "They were both killed, but the earl returned with gold and spices and rich cloth he'd captured. He never helped the widows and orphans his war made. I could understand if his castle and our town were attacked. Then it would be our duty to fight. But this was a war that didn't concern us. It was just to bring glory and riches to the earl."

"I knew there was something about him I didn't like," Matthew said.

The three of them ate the rest of the

meal in silence. The reed candle was getting short. Both Holly and Matthew helped Meg Turner clean the dishes and put away the leftover food.

They all took off their shoes and each found a soft place in the straw. Meg Turner blew out the light. In almost no time they were fast asleep.

Holly woke to the sound of a rooster crowing. She sat up and rubbed her eyes. The first pale gray light of morning was coming through the little square

windows. She had to shake Matthew before he would open his eyes. Even then it took a moment or two before he remembered where he was. Then he yawned and stretched and reached over to pick up his shirt with the cat curled up in it.

Meg Turner was up and busy stirring something in a pot on the hearthstone. "There's a well in the yard if you want to wash your face and tidy up," she said. "You should try to look your best when you reach the castle."

Holly put on her shoes, took the shirt and the cat from her brother, and went outdoors.

Matthew found his shoes and shoved his feet into them. Then he too went out into the yard.

22

Holly put the cat next to the low stone wall around the well. Albert peeked out of the shirt.

Matthew arrived as Holly took hold of the wooden bucket on the wall. "I'll help you with that pail in a minute. But first I want my shirt back. Albert can hide just as well in this tunic."

"I'd rather keep the shirt," the cat said.

"In the tunic, Matt, you look as if you belong around here, and we'll be safer," Holly said. "Besides, it would be rude to Meg Turner to take it off."

"It's itchy," Matthew said. "You're not the one who has to wear it."

"Your T-shirt is soft and white, just right to wrap a baby in," Holly persisted.

Matthew reached to grab the shirt.

"Stop!" the cat said in a low voice. "Or I'll have to take control. Don't forget. I am the Master of the Magic!"

"That's what you think." Matthew pulled the slipper from his pocket. "Whose slipper are you?"

The slipper did not move.

"Slipper," the cat commanded, "go to the castle and do what you can to help Nell Fisher. We will meet you there."

The slipper trembled. Matthew tried to hold on to it, but it wiggled out of his hand and flew away before he knew what was happening.

"Albert's right, Matt," Holly said. "We have to listen to him. I'm sorry you don't want to wear the tunic. It looks good on you. As soon as we're away from Meg Turner's house, I'll put it on. Albert can have my shirt."

Matt laughed. "You'd look silly in it." He grabbed a rope and helped Holly lower the bucket that was tied to it into the well.

Together they pulled up the bucket of cool water. The children cupped their hands and drank from them.

Holly held the cat so he could lap from the pail. Then she washed her face and ran her wet fingers through her hair.

Matthew picked up his shirt, cat and all, and carried it into the house. "No hard feelings, Albert," he said. "I had it coming to me."

Meg Turner had a bowl of porridge with honey on it ready for each of the

children and a cup of warm milk for
Albert.

When they were ready to go, she
handed Matthew a little basket. "Something to eat for the journey," she said.

Meg Turner tipped her head to one
side and looked hard at Matthew. "You
look just as handsome in that tunic as my
son did. I'm happy that I gave it to you."

23

Holly carried the cat wrapped in Matthew's T-shirt, and Matthew took charge of the lunch basket. They followed the path above the river and walked into the little town.

"Look, Matt," Holly whispered. "That man is wearing a tunic like yours."

Matthew tried not to stare. "I'm glad I still have my jeans!"

The man's pants were tied to his legs with narrow strips of cloth.

"They're better than those long baggy dresses the girls here are wearing," Holly said. "And what a job to have to braid all that hair!"

They came to an open square where a gray stone church had been built. People were filling jugs with water from a well.

When Matthew and Holly left the town, the path began to go uphill. It was hard and stony now.

They went around a bend and looked down to see the river below them.

Albert poked his head out of Matthew's shirt. "We must be on Castle Rock," he said. "I've never dared to come here before."

They sat down beside the path and ate the bread, cheese, and apples in Meg Turner's basket.

Holly held the cat while he lapped milk from a little jar with a wooden stopper.

From above came the sound of horses' hooves on the stony path.

Matthew grabbed Albert and wrapped him in his shirt. Holly jammed the stopper back into the jar and started to crunch an apple.

Three men on horseback came rattling down the hill, sending stones rolling onto the picnickers. The horses galloped on toward the town.

Holly went back to eating her apple and giving Albert his milk.

Between bites of bread and cheese, Matthew said to the cat, "I don't understand why the slipper kept doing things for both Holly and me and then, all of a sudden, it would only obey you."

"You two kept giving orders I would like to have thought of," Albert told him. "The slipper never heard me object."

"Let's not waste time talking about it," Holly said. "We have to get into the castle."

It was a long hike to the top of Castle Rock. Matthew and Holly had to step off the path so a man driving a donkey cart could get by. He was going to town to buy food for the castle.

They were out of breath when at last they came to a thick fence of pointed tree trunks. A man with a spear was guarding the heavy oak gates in the fence. He let

the people coming out of the gates pass
him. But when Holly and Matthew tried
to walk in, he barred the way with his
spear. "What do you two boys have in
that bundle?"

Albert let out a wail.

The guard stroked his beard.

Matthew opened his mouth to say
something, but his sister stepped on his
foot to stop him.

Holly had short curly hair and wore
jeans. She decided to let people here
think she was a boy. "Yesterday the earl

put our friend Lady Eleanor in front of him on his horse to bring her here. He told my brother and me there was not room for us on the horse, but that we would be welcome at Castle Garrick."

The guard started to laugh, but stopped. "It's his idea of a joke, but I'm sure it's not funny to you." He took a good look at the children. "Take that hungry baby to the cookhouse and tell Osmond, the head cook, that Ethelbert said to give you boys something to eat. Now go in and keep quiet about this. Osmond is a friend of mine and I don't want him to get into trouble." The guard raised his spear to let them walk through the gateway.

24

A wide strip of land went around the castle like a road. Holly and Matthew had to duck out of the way of two teen-aged boys riding horseback.

They came to a ditch filled with water. "That's what they call a moat," Matthew said. "Look, there's a drawbridge!"

They crossed the bridge. The iron grating on the other side was up. Holly and Matthew walked under it and through an arch in a stone wall that was thicker than any wall they'd ever seen before.

Beyond the wall was a large courtyard full of busy people and farm animals. Holly looked around. Within the courtyard she saw another moat and a drawbridge leading to an even thicker wall. Rising high on the other side of that wall was an enormous round tower.

"It was nice of Ethelbert to tell us how to get food," Holly said, "but I'm not hungry right now."

"Neither am I," her brother agreed. "Let's explore the castle."

They looked into a carpenter shop in the courtyard. A man there was sawing a tree trunk into thick boards. He put down his saw and smiled at Holly and Matthew. "Is there something I can do for you?"

"Have you seen a pretty lady in a blue dess with white daisies on it? The earl brought her to the castle yesterday."

"Everybody saw her," the carpenter

said. "We were all waiting to see what the earl would bring home from the hunt."

"Where can we find her?" Holly asked.

"The earl took her to the donjon." The man picked up his saw and went back to work.

Holly looked at her brother. "Why would he put her in the dungeon?" she whispered.

"Maybe he found out who she was," Matthew said in an even softer whisper.

Now a loud whisper came from the T-shirt Holly was carrying. "A donjon is not a dungeon!"

Holly carried the hidden cat away from the carpenter shop. "There's nobody very close to us, Matt. If Albert says anything, I'll move my lips, so people will think I'm the one who's talking."

"Did you hear that, Albert?" Matthew said.

The cat started to whisper, and Holly silently moved her lips.

"The donjon is the big strong tower in the middle of a castle," Albert told them. "The lord of a castle and his guests live in the upper part of the tower. The dungeon is in the lowest place under the tower. It is a dark, damp, rat-infested prison."

When Albert finished, Holly stopped pretending to talk and said, "I guess we'd better visit the donjon, Matt."

Matthew grinned. "The upper part of the tower."

Holly walked quickly across the busy courtyard to the drawbridge that crossed the inner moat. Her brother hurried to keep up with her.

People were walking back and forth across the bridge. Some of them seemed to be carrying something for those who lived in the tower. Two young women

had baskets of laundry. A man with an apron held a covered dish from the cookhouse. There was a peddler with a pack on his back. Servants struggled with heavy pails of water.

The guard on the bridge let all these people pass, but he stopped people who were empty-handed.

"Slow down, Holly," Matthew said. "I think it's time we went to see Osmond."

25

It was easy to find the cookhouse. Matthew and Holly just followed their noses. The smell of roasting meat came from a stone building in the courtyard. It had a high pointed roof with a hole in the center to let the smoke out. They walked through an open doorway.

A fire burned on a great stone hearth. Many different cooks were busy preparing food. Holly saw a man with a cleaver hacking up the carcass of a large animal. Another man was skinning and cutting up rabbits. He dropped them into an enormous pot. A woman was putting carrots and onions into the same pot.

Matthew was glad he didn't have to crank a spit to roast the row of geese on it. The boy who had this job worked close to the fire and was covered with sweat.

One man walked around the fire, watching how things were cooking. "You need more water in the pot," he told the woman adding vegetables to the stew.

Holly walked over to him, carrying the cat in the T-shirt. Matthew went after her.

"We're looking for Osmond," Holly said.

Albert let out a pitiful wail.

"I'm Osmond," the man told her.

Holly jiggled the cat as if he were a baby. "Ethelbert told us you would give us something to eat."

"Of course I will. You're strangers here. Any friend of Ethelbert's is a friend of mine." Osmond took a wooden platter from a pile of them on a big table. He walked around the cookhouse and loaded the platter with the nicest cuts of meat from the fire. Then he went to the big baskets of fruit that were in the shade of a tree in the courtyard. He chose the prettiest peaches and plums and put them on the platter. Finally he added a loaf of bread that had been baked in the big stone oven near the cookhouse. "How's that?"

"Wonderful! Thank you," Holly said.

Osmond gave the platter to Matthew to carry. "Don't eat it near the cook-house," he whispered. "Or everyone will be asking me for the same." He went back to his work.

Matthew carried the tray of food before him as if he were in a parade. "Hold

Albert up like a present," he told his sister.

Holly walked proudly behind Matthew holding the cat in front of her chest.

They crossed the courtyard to the inner drawbridge. The guard on the bridge let them pass and go through the gate in the tremendous wall.

Now they were in a well-kept rose garden. And right ahead was the towering donjon.

26

The guard at the door of the donjon looked at the tray of food Matthew was carrying. "It's early for dinner," he said. "Who's getting that?"

"We're taking it to Lady Eleanor of Fiswell," Matthew told him.

"Well, you'd better hurry before it gets cold. She's in the room at the top of the west tower." The guard stepped aside to let Matthew and Holly pass.

They walked into a narrow passage. There were several stairways going up from it. "I wonder which stair is to the west tower," Holly said.

Albert started to whisper. At once Holly began to move her lips and pretend to be the one who was talking.

"If I were on the ground, my nose would tell me where Nell is," the cat said. "You could follow me."

"Suppose somebody saw you?" Matthew said.

"I could run," Albert whispered. "There are lots of places to hide in a castle."

Holly was still moving her lips. She wanted to remind the cat that she and her brother could never go home if Albert left them, but Matthew said, "It's dark here. Holly will put you down." He nodded to his sister. "Go ahead, but pretend you're still carrying something in my shirt."

Holly looked around the shadowy hall. There was no one in sight. She unwrapped Albert from the T-shirt and bent down to put him on the stone floor.

The cat stretched his legs, lifted his head to sniff the air, and trotted down the passage. When he came to a stair, he stopped and sniffed all around it. Then he continued down the winding passage. Matthew and Holly went after him.

Albert stopped at another stair and began to check that one. Before he finished checking, two young men came chasing each other down the stair. The cat turned and ran back down the hall. Holly

threw the T-shirt over him and picked him up. She held him in front of her as she had before and kept walking.

The two young men were coming toward the children.

"Did you see that rat?" Matthew said to them.

"A real monster," one of them said.

The other agreed. "It was as big as a cat! Come on, Cuthbert, let's get out of here."

As soon as the young men were out of sight, Albert wiggled out of the T-shirt and jumped to the ground. He trotted along with his nose on the ground. When they came to a narrow twisting stair, he started right up.

Matthew and Holly were close behind him.

27

The stairway led to a different floor. The children followed the cat through a maze of narrow passages and past several rooms. Albert stopped at the foot of a winding staircase. Holly and Matthew heard the faint sound of voices coming from overhead.

Holly unfolded the T-shirt. The cat came over to be wrapped up. Holding the tray of food, Matthew led the way up the stairs.

They went higher. The voices were louder. The stair ended at a door.

Holly tapped on the door. It was opened by the earl!

He stared at the two children. Then

he smiled. "You're here at last! I was afraid something had happened to you." He pinched Holly's cheek.

Holly could feel the cat's heart pounding under the T-shirt. Her heart began to pound too.

"Now that you're here," the earl said, "the lady will be happy." He looked at the food. "How lucky that you brought something for her to eat. She's not used to the castle food and hasn't touched a crumb in all the time she has been here." He opened the door wide for them to go in. Then he went out and shut the door behind him.

They were in a room with windows set high in the walls. Nell Fisher and two other ladies were seated at a table piled high with cloth, sewing.

Nell was even prettier than they remembered.

"Ow! I just stuck myself with this dratted needle." Nell Fisher stood up and let her sewing fall on the floor. She ran over to the children and hugged them. "I'm so glad to see you. This is a terrible place. I always thought it would be fun to see how the fine ladies live. But it's boring! I don't know what I would have done without Elspeth and Selma. They haven't eaten because I wouldn't, and they've been sewing all day just to make me a present."

"Eat!" Nell Fisher commanded the ladies. She grabbed a slice of meat from the platter. "M-m-m-m. I'm starved!"

Matthew carried the tray of food over to the two ladies and placed it on the table near them. They put down their sewing and began to eat.

"Nell," Holly whispered. "Here's Albert."

Nell Fisher looked at the bundle of T-shirt and cat. "Give him to me." She took Albert and his wrappings and went to get another piece of meat from the tray.

"I didn't know you had a baby, Eleanor," Elspeth said.

Nell Fisher didn't answer. She carried Albert and the T-shirt to a large pile of straw in one corner of the room. "I'd better give him his dinner in bed."

"There must be something terribly wrong with him," Selma whispered. The two ladies clucked their tongues in sympathy.

119

28

Nell went back to the tray of food. "Come and join us. There's enough for everybody," she told the children. She turned to the ladies. "These are my friends Holly and Matthew."

"Fine-looking boys," Selma said.

"Yes," Elspeth agreed. "But I'll have to work on those leggings the little one is wearing. I'm sure I can improve them. I love to sew."

When they had all finished eating, the two ladies picked up their sewing again.

The door opened and the earl came into the room. He walked over to Matthew. "Clench your fist, lad!" He felt Matthew's arm. "Splendid! Tomorrow you can join me in a little expedition to punish the scoundrel from Castle Brandon who's been hunting in my forest."

Holly felt cold all over. She remembered what had happened to Meg Turner's son.

"The little one can serve you as a page, my lady," the earl told Nell Fisher. He turned and left the room.

Suddenly Holly caught sight of the toe of a red bedroom slipper poking out from under a pile of cloth on the table. She quietly took the slipper and carried it over to the pile of straw. "Master of the Magic, do your stuff!" she whispered, and shoved the slipper into the folded T-shirt.

Albert stuck his black, whiskery face out of the T-shirt. He was holding the red bedroom slipper in his mouth.

Elspeth took one look at the cat and let out a hair-raising scream. She hurried to open the door. Selma jumped to her feet and followed her. Both ladies ran down the winding stair as fast as they could in their long dresses.

Albert placed the slipper on the floor. "Slipper, get ready to take all four of us to Brooklyn! Hurry!"

Nothing happened.

They could hear heavy footsteps coming up the stair.

The cat sniffed the slipper. "Something's happened to it. The slipper doesn't smell of magic any more!"

29

The herb mixture must have worn off the slipper, Holly thought. Now there was no way for them to go home again.

The footsteps on the stairs were coming closer.

Matthew picked up the slipper. "Of course it isn't magic! This isn't my beat-up old slipper. It's brand new, and it's not even corduroy. It's velvet!"

Nell Fisher grabbed the slipper and lifted the hem of her long dress. She was wearing two red slippers. She took one off and gave it to Matthew. "Is this what you're looking for?" She put on the other slipper.

Matthew placed the slipper on the floor. "Do your best, Slipper!"

The earl was at the door now.

Holly wished Matthew had let Albert work the magic.

The earl stood in the doorway with his fist in the air, but the slipper had cast a spell, and he couldn't get into the room.

The slipper became bigger and bigger until there was room for Holly and Matthew to sit with Nell Fisher between them holding Albert on her lap.

When the slipper rose in the air, the earl rushed into the room. By that time the slipper had become small enough to go through the lattice of the window. It soared higher and higher to leave the castle behind and race forward through time.

"Nobody told me that slipper was magic," Nell Fisher said. "When I found it on the floor, I tried it on. It was so much better than the awful things I was wearing that Elspeth and Selma decided to copy it and make me a new pair. Selma finished hers first. I was wearing Matthew's slipper while Elspeth worked on hers."

Nell Fisher admired the tunic. Matthew took it off and gave it to her. He put on his T-shirt. It had cat hairs on it and was itchier than the tunic.

The window of Holly's room in the Dorritys' house was still wide open. The slipper flew into her bedroom and landed on the floor. As soon as Holly and Matthew climbed out, they returned to their usual size. The slipper was still tiny. It rose up and sailed out the window with Albert and Nell Fisher.

"I wonder where the slipper is taking them," Matthew said. "I didn't hear Albert give any commands."

Holly thought about this. "The slipper seems to have a mind of its own now. Look what it did to the earl!"

30

Matthew changed his shirt, and Holly combed her hair. They went downstairs. Mr. Dorrity was busy with the crossword puzzle, and Mrs. Dorrity was working in her garden.

"What do you think the herbs were that got smeared on to my slipper?" Matthew asked. "Maybe there's some of the mixture still on the floor."

"Let's go see." Holly and Matthew started up the stairs. They met Albert on the way down. "Where's Nell Fisher?" Holly asked.

"She just got a job in the circus," the cat told them. "She did a few acrobatic tricks and proved she could ride on an elephant's head. The manager said she was the prettiest acrobat he'd ever seen.

"By the way, Matt, I put your slipper with the other one under your bed. It needs a rest, and I need some of your grandmother's leftovers."

Albert ran downstairs to the kitchen.